THAT NIGHT WITH MY BEST FRIEND'S BROTHER

(PREQUEL NOVELLA TO FALLING FOR MY BEST FRIEND'S BROTHER)

J. S. COOPER & HELEN COOPER

Thank you for reading
That Night with My Best Friend's Brother.

This is the prequel novella to the full-length book
Falling For My Best Friend's Brother.

Join my <u>MAILING LIST</u>
to be notified of all my new releases.

About That Night with My Best Friend's Brother

I want more than one night with Aiden Taylor.

Aiden Taylor is my best friend's brother. He's sexy, charming and drop dead gorgeous. He also doesn't know I exist as anything other than his little sister's best friend.

However, I'm determined to change that. I'm Alice Waldron. Twenty-two, spunky, and adventurous. I'm willing to do whatever it takes for Aiden to notice me. And Liv, my best friend, is determined to help me as well.

The only problem is that I have a small secret. A secret that could make my getting together with Aiden Taylor very complicated. A secret that could make more than one night with Aiden nothing more than a dream.

NOTE: This novella is a free steamy prequel to the full-length standalone novel Falling For My Best Friend's Brother, that will be released at the end of February. This novella will also be included in the full-length book when it is released, so you can read it first as a free download or you can read it as part of the novel on release day.

Table of Contents

Prologue

I have a piece of advice for you. Never fall in love with your best friend's brother. Don't fall for his boyish smile or his gorgeous big blue eyes. Don't fall for his bulging biceps or his arrogant smirk. There's nothing good that can come from falling for him. Trust me, I know. My name's Alice and I have the biggest crush on my best friend Liv's brother, Aiden. He's everything I want in a man, aside from the fact that he's brooding, overprotective, annoying, and too devastatingly handsome for his own good. Aiden Taylor was everything I wanted in a man, but he was the one man that I couldn't have. He was the one man I couldn't let myself be with. I couldn't afford to date him and then have everything go wrong. Liv was my best friend and like my sister and if I dated Aiden and it didn't work out, I was scared that would ruin our relationship as well. Plus, I was scared what would happen if the truth came out. You see, there are secrets about Aiden and me that nobody knows about. Secrets that neither of us want found out.

Chapter One

"Alice, you need to learn to take your own advice." Liv wriggled her eyebrows at me as she changed the channel on the TV. Her brown doe-like eyes gazed at me with a challenge and I stifled a groan. I knew that look well. As well I should, as I was the one who had taught it to her.

"What advice is that?" I said as I casually picked up the bowl of popcorn from the coffee table and sat back. I took a couple of kernels and popped them into my mouth, enjoying the buttery sweetness as I waited for her to say the words I was dreading to hear.

"You need to have a one-night stand with Aiden." She grinned at me and I groaned. "Don't groan at me, Alice." She grabbed some popcorn and sat back on the new tan leather couch we'd recently bought.

"Careful how you're eating," I said in a proper voice. "We don't want butter on the new couch." I laughed as she made a face at me. "Also, I'm not going to have a one-night stand with your brother." I looked at the TV screen as my heart raced. I'm not going to lie, I've thought about sleeping (and when I say sleeping, I mean anything but sleeping) with Aiden for years. But he's never seen me as anything more than his little sister's best friend. And even then I don't think he really paid much attention to me. Well, technically that's not really true. There was one night that he saw me as more than 'silly little Alice'. There was one night that he saw me as a woman, but I'm not going to talk about that.

"I didn't think I would have a one-night stand either but I did and look at me now." Liv muted the TV and looked at me. I watched as she fluffed her long brown hair and twirled a loose wave around her finger. "Who would have thought Xander and I would be—"

"Yeah, yeah, I get it," I said, cutting her off. I really wasn't in the mood to hear about how wonderful her relationship was with Xander, her boyfriend. Xander James was handsome, sexy, rich and supposedly really good in bed—and with his tongue. I'd been hearing about Xander James for the last few months and I just didn't get how one man could be so perfect. I was so happy for Liv; she is my best friend in the world, after all, but if I'm honest, I'm a bit envious as well. I want a guy who will sweep me off of my feet and fall head-over-heels in love with me. I want a guy who will look at me like I'm the only woman on earth. Right now, I get the guys who look at me like I'm a discounted piece of steak or like I'm some sort of free entertainment. Hello, I'm not your personal stripper (unless you're dropping thousands of dollars and don't expect to be able to touch me) and no, I won't dress up in my high school Hooters outfit for you (again). The fact was that Liv had hit the boyfriend lottery with Xander and I was scraping the bottom of the barrel.

"Am I being annoying?" Liv frowned as she gazed at me, her brown eyes crinkling in concern that she was acting like that friend who we all love to hate. That friend who finds her man, falls in love and can't stop going on and on about it. I didn't mind her going on about it, normally. I just didn't want her to talk about her love life in the same breath with Aiden's name. Not when he was someone I'd been craving for years.

"No, Liv." I smiled widely, though my insides were grumbling that yes, she was being annoying. No one wanted to hear about their best friend's perfect lover every day. Though I suppose I'm being unfair, since Xander is really quite far from perfect. I smiled to myself wickedly as I thought about their relationship.

"What are you smiling about?" Liv's eyes narrowed and she moved closer to me. "Is there something you're not telling me, Alice?"

"Maybe." I grinned and started laughing as she sat there staring at me with a perplexed expression. I started to feel guilty when Liv's face started to look worried. I knew then that she was starting to feel bad and most probably overthinking everything. That was Liv's biggest downfall and one of the reasons that I loved her. She was way too sensitive. She took on every emotion and she was always super worried and anxious if she thought she was causing pain to anyone. "I'm just joking, Liv." I leaned forward to squeeze her arm. "I'm happy for you and Xander. You deserved to find love."

"I know." She smiled and then sighed. "But I want you to find love as well. I want you to be as happy as I am."

"I'll meet someone soon. I mean, we can even go out tomorrow night if you're down. I might meet a nice guy."

"Xander says he doesn't want me to go to any nightclubs with you anymore." She bit her lower lip and I stared at her.

"I know that you aren't allowing Xander to dictate what you do and don't do, right?" I frowned. How dare he ban her from going to nightclubs with me, like I was some sort of bad influence?

"Of course not." She giggled. "We just can't announce it to him."

"You're not going to lie to him, are you?" I made a face. If she lied and he found out, he would hate me.

"No, of course not. I'm just not going to volunteer where we're going."

"Really?" I looked at her face carefully and then I saw the glint in her eyes. "You're such a liar, Liv. You're going to totally tell Xander and then you're going to have him tell Aiden and it's going to be all World War III up in the club and we're going to be banned for life."

"Just call him, Alice." She groaned. "Please."

"No." I shook my head and stood up. "I'm going to get some ice cream. Do you want anything?"

"No." She jumped up as well. "Why won't you call him? You're just being silly. Explain to him that you didn't want to kiss Scott."

"I'm not calling him." My face reddened as I remembered the look in Aiden's eyes as I'd kissed his brother a couple of months ago. He'd looked shocked and I'd felt my stomach drop as our eyes met. It was just my luck. I hadn't even wanted to kiss Scott, but I'd let him kiss me, just so I could see if there was a spark. I wanted to explain to Aiden that it had been a mistake, but I was too ashamed to tell him anything. Especially given our past history together.

"Alice." Liv sighed and pursed her lips.

"Don't 'Alice' me, Liv." I rolled my eyes at her, starting to feel frustrated. "You wouldn't have called, either."

"Maybe not." She shook her head at me and we both paused and looked down at her pocket as her phone rang.

"Get it." I walked away from her. "Your obnoxious Prince Charming is waiting for you."

"He's not obnoxious," she protested as she pulled her phone out of her pocket. And then she giggled. "Well, maybe he's slightly obnoxious," she admitted and then answered the phone. "Hello," she said softly in her 'I'm a princess, come and save me' voice and I hurried down the corridor and into my bedroom.

***

I grabbed my laptop, jumped onto my bed and pulled up Facebook. I typed 'Aiden Taylor' quickly in search and my heart froze as unfamiliar photos popped onto the screen. Had Aiden unfriended me? I swallowed hard, my heart beating fast as I refreshed the page.

"Oh my God," I groaned as I realized I'd typed in 'Tyler' instead of 'Taylor'. I quickly backspaced and deleted and changed it to the correct spelling. I felt a huge rush of relief escape me as Aiden's familiar photo crossed my screen. I clicked on his photos to see if he had any new pictures and my heart stopped again when I noticed some girl called

Elizabeth Jeffries had left a comment that said, "Can't wait to see you this weekend". I clicked on her name, but her profile was private and I couldn't see anything else. Who the hell was Elizabeth Jeffries? Was she his girlfriend? Did he love her? Ugh! My head was spinning with questions as my stomach churned. I quickly went to Google and typed her name in and looked to see if I could find anything else about her online. That was what I hated and loved about the internet. It was so easy to stalk—I mean, "research" — people, but the flipside of that was that people could research me, too. I wasn't happy with the fact that when people typed 'Alice Waldron' into Google, a photo I'd submitted to a weight loss competition came up on a weight loss website, along with my goal weight (which I had not reached). I also wasn't proud of the fact that you could also see my posts on a celebrity gossip blog rating different Hollywood celebrities. I'd contacted Google and asked them to remove those websites from search, but they hadn't responded.

"Alice, what are you doing?" Liv walked into my room with two different tops in her hands.

"Research," I mumbled as I looked up at her, debating whether or not I should ask her if she knew who Elizabeth Jeffries was.

"Research for what?" Liv plopped down onto my bed and I tried to adjust my laptop so that she couldn't see it. It was one thing to be a stalker, but it was another thing to be caught stalking. Especially when it involves your best friend's brother.

"Work," I lied and avoided her thoughtful gaze.

"What do you have to research for work?" she questioned, her voice doubtful. And who could blame her? I was an assistant at a real estate firm. There wasn't much that I did in the office, let alone had to do from home.

"What are you, a FBI agent?" I snapped, feeling peeved that she was questioning me.

"Okay, so what has Aiden been up to recently?" She laughed and I looked up at her. "I'm not dumb, Alice. I obviously can guess that your research is about my big bro. You've never had to do research for work before. Not that you've mentioned to me, anyway."

"Boo to my easy job." I laughed and handed my laptop over to Liv. "Do you know who Elizabeth Jeffries is, by any chance?"

"Elizabeth who?" she asked in a confused voice.

"I'm guessing that's a no." I sighed. "Do you know if Aiden is dating anyone?"

"Not that he's told me." She frowned. "Why? Does it say he's in a relationship on Facebook?"

"Not exactly." I shook my head. "But this whore Elizabeth is commenting on his wall."

"What? A prostitute?" Liv's eyes widened and she looked down at the computer to see what I was talking about. "How do you know she's a working girl?"

"Oh," I said meekly, feeling bad for calling my unknown nemesis and enemy a whore. "I don't know if she's really a whore, Liv. Keep up." I rolled my eyes at her.

"What?" She looked up at me. "You're confusing me. Is my brother dating a whore or not?"

"Oh my gosh, Liv." I groaned. "I was looking at Aiden's profile on Facebook and some *girl* called Elizabeth commented on his wall saying she can't wait to see him this weekend and I called her a whore because I'm jealous and *I* want to see him this weekend," I explained feebly. "And if you didn't have your head in the clouds, you would have understood what I was talking about."

"Oh, I get it." She giggled. "She's not a whore, like she's hooking up for money, but she's a whore in that she's a ho because she's after your man."

"I prefer my explanation." I giggled. "Yours makes me sound like a psycho. I can't call her a ho because she's after my man because he's not my man."

"Alice," she groaned, "you're super confusing me."

"You're super confusing *me*." I made a face. "Now do you know her or not?"

"I've never heard of her before in my life," Liv said and handed me back the laptop. "Do you want me to call Aiden and see what's up?"

"I don't know. Do you think that will be obvious?" I asked her as I gazed down at Aiden's profile again. "Oh shit." I groaned out loud as I gave Elizabeth's comment a like. "I just liked her post on his wall. What should I do?"

"Unlike it quickly," Liv said as she shook her head. "And then like a different post, so if Aiden gets notifications, he will see you have a like somewhere."

"Ugh, he's going to know I was Facebook-stalking him." I sighed. "I'm such a loser."

"Alice, it's fine." She jumped off of the bed. "I'm sure he won't think anything of it."

"You think so?"

"I know so. Guys don't analyze Facebook likes and comments like we do." She smiled at me encouragingly. "He most probably won't even notice that you liked anything."

"Yeah, I guess so." I nodded hesitantly, my heart racing in fear. Liv was talking as if she knew what she was talking about and she most probably thought she knew everything about men now that she was dating Xander, but I knew that she didn't really know that much. I mean, she hadn't been dating Xander for very long and I was the one who had given her all her dating advice up until she started dating him. So essentially, Liv was giving me the advice I would have given her and in all honesty, I had absolutely no idea what I'd been talking about when I was the one giving advice.

***

Have you ever done something you know you shouldn't do? Like sending a guy a Facebook message in the middle of the night, when you knew you absolutely should not be sending him a message? And doing it sober, no less. Drunk messaging and drunk dialing can be forgiven, but sober messaging is done by fools, like me.

I knew I shouldn't send Aiden a message. I knew I should wait for him to contact me. That's what all the rules say, right? If a guy is interested, he'll contact you. I knew that, but I was worried that he would think I had something for Scott—his brother. He caught me kissing Scott. Well, really he caught Scott kissing me, but ever since that night, Aiden has acted like I'm a leper or invisible. And I don't even *like* Scott, which he should know, but you know men. They can be weird and stupid and totally obnoxious and arrogant and so that was why I sent Aiden a Facebook message at 11 p.m.

Hi Aiden, it's me, Alice. Hehe, obviously as it's from my Facebook page. Just wanted to say Hi. So Hi. And then I hit send. And then I fell back on my pillow and groaned. Why oh why had I sent a Facebook message to Aiden? Ugh. Then I heard a small ding and sat up again. Someone had sent me a message. I quickly looked at my Facebook account.

Hi Alice. That was all Aiden had said in his reply, but I felt as giddy as a drunk mouse as I stared at the screen. He had replied to me. He didn't hate me! I quickly clicked on my profile to see what photo I had up as my profile photo. I groaned as I saw myself grinning like a fool, my medium-length blonde hair looking messy and my blue eyes looking squinted. This was not the photo I wanted Aiden to be staring at as he typed back to me.

You're up late, I typed back quickly. I know, I know, I really shouldn't have sent another message. He hadn't exactly been enthusiastic in his response, but I didn't care. The fact that he had responded, period, was good enough for me.

It's 11pm. Not exactly last call. I rolled my eyes at his response.

I don't go drinking every night, so I wouldn't know, I typed back quickly. *Asshole.*

Just a few times a week? Only when Brock and Jock are available?

Haha. Very Funny. I made a face. Brock and Jock were twins that I had hired to pose as boyfriends to Liv and me in order to make Xander jealous when things hadn't been going too well for them. It hadn't worked out very well, and Brock and Jock hadn't fooled anyone into believing that they were our boyfriends.

What are you doing up so late? Looking to get into trouble? My heart stopped as I read his words. Was he trying to pick me up?

What kind of trouble? I typed back quickly.

You tell me.

What are you asking me, Aiden?

Nothing. I was just joking.

Oh okay. What are you doing?

About to hit the sack. I have a big meeting at work tomorrow.

Oh okay. Disappointment filled me. Tonight wasn't going to be the night that Aiden Taylor professed his love for me.

Sweet Dreams, Alice. Don't do anything I wouldn't do.

That might be hard.

I'm well aware of that. :)

What does that mean?

What do you think it means?

I'm not 16 anymore.

I'm glad to hear it.

It was an honest mistake. I lied. It hadn't been a mistake at all.

I know. You told me.

I got confused about whose bed was whose.

Sure, you did.

What does that mean? Sure, you did.

Alice, sweet dreams.

We should talk about this Aiden. I don't want you thinking anything that you shouldn't be thinking.

That was a long time ago, Alice. I'm over it.

Fine. Good Night. I closed my laptop and jumped out of bed, feeling antsy. What did he mean he was over it? Was he still mad at me? Was he angry? Was he trying to tell me that he was over me and letting me know that I had no shot with him? I groaned as I walked to the kitchen and heard Liv and Xander whispering and doing heaven knows what in the living room.

"Get a room, guys!" I shouted into the living room with a snarl, suddenly feeling upset and angry at the both of them.

"Alice?" Liv sounded surprised and I heard her get up off of the couch and walk into the kitchen. "Everything okay?"

"I'm fine. Just wondering why you guys think it's okay to make out in our joint living room," I said churlishly as I opened the fridge. "Isn't your boyfriend a millionaire or something? Do you guys have to make out in our living room, like some randy teenagers?"

"We weren't making out," Liv said simply. "We were watching a movie."

"So why did I hear whispering and kissing?"

"You heard kissing?" Liv raised an eyebrow at me. "Xander asked me to pass him the popcorn and I told him to get his own," she explained and studied my face. "What's going on, Alice?"

"Nothing." I bit my lower lip, my face hot with shame. "Sorry."

"There's nothing to be sorry about." She continued to stand there. "Are you sad about Aiden?"

"He's just a jerk." I groaned again as I pulled out the carton of chocolate milk. "I don't know why he gets to me so much."

"Because you like him." She smiled.

"Yeah, I guess so." I poured a tall glass and then looked for some cookies. My stomach was in knots and I needed a sugar high to make me feel better.

"It's fine, Alice," she continued. "He's just being an ass. He'll come around and he'll forget that silly little kiss."

"That's not everything," I said softly as I pulled out my purple box of Cadbury Fingers. They were my expensive treat to myself. They were more expensive than regular cookies because they were imported from England, but I loved my sticks of biscuit covered by milk chocolate. They were worth going broke for.

"What do you mean, that's not everything?" Liv stood behind me and as I turned around, her brown eyes looked cautious. "You didn't have sex with Scott, did you?"

"What?" My voice rose and my jaw dropped. "Hell no. Of course I didn't sleep with Scott. How could you think that?"

"Well, you're acting funny," she said with a frown. "What else don't I know, Alice?"

"Ahem." Xander walked into the kitchen and cleared his throat. "I've put the movie on hold, but I'm wondering if I should just leave?" He looked at me and then at Liv. "It seems like you guys need to talk?"

"Thanks." I nodded and smiled at him weakly.

"No." Liv frowned and then gave me a look. "You don't have to leave."

"Are you sure?" He stood there with a smug smile on his face. "I don't mind, and it seems like Alice really needs to talk." He looked at me again and I stood there with my heart in my throat. I couldn't look at Liv. I was scared she was going to tell Xander he could stay. Which would mean that she was officially choosing him over me. Which would not be cool. I was her best friend. I had first dibs on her time. If she told him he could stay, I was going to feel very, very sad.

"If you don't mind," Liv said and walked over and gave him a kiss on the cheek. "I'll make it up to you." My shoulders relaxed at her words. She wasn't choosing Xander over me. Yet.

"I'll hold you to that," he said in a silky smooth voice and I looked away as he pulled her mouth to his and kissed her firmly. Oh how I wished Aiden would grab me like that and kiss me possessively. "Feel better, Alice."

"Thanks." I nodded and chugged my chocolate milk.

"Alice, I'm going to walk Xander to the door then I'll be back." Liv looked at me. "Pour us two glasses of Merlot. I think tonight's going to be a long night."

"Okay." I nodded and smiled. I wasn't sure how I'd gotten so lucky as to get Liv as a best friend, but I vowed to myself that I would never take her for granted. I looked in the cupboard for some wine glasses and a bottle of wine. I then opened the fridge and took out some French bread and brie, that I had not bought, and sliced the bread and put it in the mini toaster oven that we had. A couple of minutes later Liv walked back into the kitchen and I tensed slightly. I was worried that she was going to be mad at me for making her send Xander home.

"Yummy, you're toasting the French bread?" She sidled up next to me and grinned.

"Yup, and I took out the brie, too." I looked over at her. "I hope that's okay."

"Of course." She laughed. "I got chocolate as well."

"Yay."

"It's dark, so it's good for us." She pulled out her bar of chocolate from the fridge. It was Lindt dark chocolate with mint and I grinned. It was the only dark chocolate I liked because it didn't taste all gritty and bitter. The mint in this bar made the chocolate taste creamy and delicious. Almost as sinful as real milk chocolate.

"I'm sorry I made you send Xander home." I made a face as I turned the slices of French bread over so that they could be toasted on both sides. Our toaster was poorly made and it never seemed to toast the bread evenly on both sides.

"It's fine." She rubbed my shoulder. "I'm not going to just let you suffer; besides, he knows us both well enough to know that I couldn't just sit there while you were upset. He knows you're my best friend and—love it or hate it—he has to deal with it."

"He hates me?" I opened the fridge and pulled the butter out.

"No." She shook her head and laughed. "I think he hates, well, not hates, more like dislikes the fact that when we're together we can be a bit immature."

"Immature?" My jaw dropped. "He thinks I'm immature?"

"He thinks we're both a bit childish." She giggled. "I told him he was wrong, but you have to admit we do have a tendency to act like teenagers sometimes."

"I take offense to that." I laughed and then shook my head. "And it's not all the time, it's just sometimes."

"That's what I told him. Everyone is entitled to act young when they want."

"Exactly, and we're only 22." I placed the bread on a plate with the cheese. "I'll take the food and you can bring the wine and the glasses."

"Okay." She nodded in agreement and followed me into the living room. I have to admit I felt bad when I saw the lit candles on the coffee table, with Liv's favorite cream faux angora wool blanket strewn on the couch. There was also a single red rose on the table next to the candle.

"Oh, man." I looked back at her with an apologetic look. "I ruined a romantic night."

"It's fine." She smiled at me.

"He gave you a red rose?" My heart had a sudden ache. "That's so sweet."

"He said that he's never given a woman a red rose before." She nodded. "He said that he vowed never to give a woman red roses until he met the woman he loved."

"Oh my God, that is so sweet." I sighed. "Argh, why does he have to be so perfect?"

"He told me that he couldn't believe that he was so lucky," she squeaked out with a huge grin. "He told me that I made him a believer and that he doesn't want to spend a day or night without me."

"Wow, thanks for making me feel even worse." I groaned. "How sweet is he?" I sighed. "I shouldn't have made him leave. Call him and tell him to come back. We can talk tomorrow."

"No, we will talk tonight." She sat down on the couch and opened the bottle of wine. "I want to know what's going on, Alice."

"It's not important. Call Xander and tell him to come back so that you can have hot sex and tell him you don't want to spend a night without him either."

"Alice." She giggled. "He can go without sex for one night. Might make him miss me even more."

"You're silly." I giggled. "Though, what's that saying? 'Treat them mean, keep them keen'?"

"'Make them wait, get the hate'?" she said with a laugh.

"Or, 'Give them blue balls, get eaten by Jaws'," I said.

"No, no, I've got it." She laughed. "'Make them jack off, make them cough'."

"Cough? Eh?" I started laughing harder. "That makes no sense."

"Make them cough up a big diamond ring." She laughed and I watched as her head fell back and her eyes watered up in tears.

"That's stupid." I continued laughing and sipped at my wine. "But thanks for making me laugh."

"Of course." She grinned and then looked me directly in the eyes. "Now tell me, what haven't you told me?"

I took another sip of wine, swallowed and took a deep breath. "I lost my virginity to Aiden," I said softly and I watched as Liv spat her wine onto her lap in shock.

Chapter Two

You know that saying. The one about a watched phone never rings? Well, it's not true. My phone has been ringing off the hook all morning. The only person who hasn't called me is the one person I want to call me. I've had calls from the local satellite company telling me I needed to switch from cable. I told them I'll switch if they can promise that I only have to pay a dollar a month for the next ten years. She cursed at me and then hung up when I told her I wanted a new 50" TV as well to sweeten the deal. I also had a call from my dentist. Well, his receptionist called to tell me that I'd missed my last two appointments and that I needed to come in for a cleaning. Yeah, right. Not anytime soon, Dr. Rosenberg. The last time I needed a cleaning, I had several cavities that needed to be filled. I'm still paying off my portion of that bill. Thanks for nothing, $300-a-month insurance bill. And of course, I also had a call from my dear old grandma, wanting to know when I was getting married and giving her grandbabies. I told her she can go to the local park and see some babies there, but she wasn't amused. So yes, I've had a lot of calls today, but none from Aiden, the man I really wanted to hear from.

Aiden Taylor is Liv's oldest brother. I've known him since I was a little kid and I've had a crush on him since I was ten and he was sixteen. Not that he ever gave me the time of day. I was always his annoying kid-sister's best friend. Well, almost always. There was one time that I was more than that. One time that we shared a moment that I've relived every day of my life since it happened. Only it's not something I can talk about with him. Not at all. I'm lucky that he still talks to me after that little episode. And we're the only ones who know. Well, we were the only ones who knew. Until very recently. I didn't tell Liv at the time and she's my best friend. I wanted to tell her. I really, really did, but how do you tell someone something like that? How do you tell your best friend that her brother was right and that you're the bad influence that no one wants in their kids' lives? I guess I should be grateful that Aiden never said anything. I suppose he was embarrassed as well or something. I mean, it's not exactly something you shout out to the world. "Hey, Liv, I slept with your best friend. In fact, I took her virginity." Yeah, he didn't say that. And I didn't tell Liv, either. How could I tell her that I'd crept into her brother's bed with the hopes of seducing him? How could I tell her that we'd made love and that it had been the best night of my life? I didn't know how to tell her and then I'd felt too guilty to bring it up, but now she knew and I honestly didn't feel better. I knew now that the one person I really needed to talk to about that night was the one man who wanted nothing to do with me.

"Alice!" Liv shouted as she walked into the apartment. "Where are you?"

"I'm in the living room!" I shouted back and then lowered my voice. "Why are we shouting, by the way?"

"I've had a brilliant idea." Her eyes were sparkling as she ran into the living room. She clapped her hands and did a little dance as she grinned at me, her enthusiasm for her idea refusing to be quelled.

"What's the idea?" My eyes narrowed as she finally stood still.

"I have a way for you to start talking to Aiden again."

"Oh?" My heart raced at her words. I looked up at her and studied her face carefully. "A good idea or a harebrained idea?"

"Alice." She pouted, her eyes looking at me wickedly. "Since when have I had harebrained ideas?"

"Since you became my best friend." I giggled and shook my head at her. Unfortunately it was true. We both seemed to have spur-of-the-moment ideas and plans that always seemed to get us into trouble. To be fair to Liv, I was the one who usually had the really stupid ideas, but Liv had been giving me a run for my money lately.

"We're going to join a flag football team."

"Say what?" I frowned.

"Flag football," she said excitedly. "Xander was telling me about it. He's going to be on it, too."

"Okay," I said, not feeling as excited. "How is this going to help me get Aiden?"

"He's going to be playing on the same team." She grinned. "It's going to be perfect."

"I don't know about this, Liv." I chewed on my lower lip. "Do you really think me playing football is going to win any guys? I'm not exactly the queen of anything sporty."

"Trust me." She grabbed my hands. "That's not the only plan I have. That's just step one."

"Step one?" I groaned, but my stomach was doing flip-flops in excitement. I wasn't a huge football fan, but if joining a team meant I would get to see Aiden weekly, then I was all for it.

"Oh yeah, baby." She grinned. "I've come up with a surefire way to make sure you and my brother get together." The look on her face looked so satisfied and excited that I held in my second groan. I didn't want to rain on her parade, but I'd also had a surefire plan once and it had blown up in my face.

"What's your surefire plan?" I asked weakly. There were times that I didn't love that I had rubbed off on Liv so much. When we were younger, Liv was innocent and quiet and I was the rabble-rouser, always looking to get into something. I always had a plan or a scheme and they had never worked out as I'd planned them to.

"You're going to go to the flag football games with me and Xander. You're going to look pretty and flirt with all the attractive single men. You're going to be nice, but not overly friendly to Aiden. You're going to let him see what he's been missing all these years."

"You think he's even going to care or notice?"

"I'm positive of the fact." She grinned. "Now that I know what happened between the two of you, I understand the dynamic between you both a lot better."

"Really?"

"Oh yes." She nodded. "I always wondered why he used to look at you with such protectiveness, but also with a kind of possessiveness and jealousy."

"He treats you the same way." I rolled my eyes, but my hopes were rising.

"Nope." She laughed. "Yes, he is overprotective and a bit of a jerk, but he's never acted jealous when I've talked about another guy and he's never acted possessive or upset when he's seen me with another guy. He couldn't care less. You know he told me he's glad I'm dating Xander because now Xander can worry about me."

"Yeah, but he's just saying that. He loves you."

"Yes, he loves me. I'm his sister." She grinned. "But he has feelings for you as well. Feelings that are about more than being your big brother. I bet he's confused."

"Confused about what?"

"He's confused that he had this night with you all those years ago that he enjoyed, but feels guilty about it and now he's not sure what to do."

"You think so?" I asked hopefully.

"Yeah, I really do." She nodded. "The problem is he still sees you as a teenager. You need to show him you're a woman now."

"And flag football will do that?"

"You, in some short-shorts running down a field, with hot guys chasing you as your long blonde hair flies in the wind, will do that." She grinned again. "Come on, Alice, you know how guys are."

"But what about Scott and what about my Facebook message?"

"Ah, forget them. They mean nothing."

"You think so?"

"I know so." She nodded.

"What do you know?" Xander's voice filled the room and I groaned.

"What are you doing here?" I asked accusingly and he laughed.

"Nice to see you too, Alice. I'm taking my girlfriend out to dinner. Is that okay with you?"

"Yeah, that's fine." I looked at Liv and she grinned.

"He was parking the car," she explained. "I left the door open for him to come in."

"Oh, okay. I was wondering if you gave him a key already."

"Would you have a problem with that?" Xander teased me. "I don't see anything wrong with that."

"I'm sure you wouldn't." I shook my head at him.

"I bet you wouldn't mind if Aiden had a key, though." He winked at me. "Maybe this time *he* can be the one to slip into *your* bedroom and bed."

"Liv!" I screamed as my face went hot. "You told Xander?"

"Xander." Liv turned to him with angry eyes. "What are you thinking?"

"What?" he asked innocently.

"Why would you tell Alice that I told you?" She sighed and looked at me with apologetic eyes. "I'm sorry, but he wanted to know what was so important that I'd kick him out last night."

"So you told him?" My jaw dropped. "I can't believe you told Xander that I lost my virginity to Aiden."

"You had sex with Aiden?" Xander's voice sounded shocked and my heart froze as I looked into Liv's eyes.

"You didn't know?" I frowned at him and then looked back at Liv.

"I didn't tell him everything." She sighed. "I didn't want to tell him everything. I just told him that you slipped into Aiden's bed one night and kissed him."

"Sex is a bit more than a kiss." Xander laughed and looked at me. "Well, well, well, Alice Waldron, the more I learn about you, the more intriguing you become."

"Argh. Whatever." I groaned and blushed again.

"Now, I need to know exactly what went down." He laughed and looked at Liv. "And I thought *we* got together under crazy circumstances."

"Well, at least you guys got together." I sighed. "Aiden didn't give me the time of day after our night together."

"It wasn't exactly the same, though, was it, Alice?" Liv spoke softly. "I mean, he didn't know it was you at first."

"Don't remind me." I groaned and put my face in my hands. "I'm so embarrassed. I should just forget everything. There's no way that Aiden will ever be able to get past that incident."

"You never know," Liv said and beamed up at Xander as he kissed her cheek and rubbed her back. I wanted to gag at how lovey-dovey they looked. "What do you think, Xander?"

"I think I need to know exactly what happened." He looked at me and his green eyes turned from laughing to a more serious expression. "I know you might be embarrassed, but trust me I can tell you if it's as bad as you think or if it's not as bad as you think."

"I'm just embarrassed." I looked down at the ground.

"It's not as bad as hooking up at a wedding with a stranger," Liv said.

"Yeah, it's not as bad as going back to a strange man's hotel room," Xander continued in a serious voice. "And then nicknaming him Mr. Tongue."

"Xander." Liv hit him in the shoulder.

"Don't you mean Mr. Tongue?" He grinned at her.

"I think she means Mr. Miracle Tongue." I laughed.

"Whatever." Liv blushed. "You're both gross."

"That's not what you said this morning," Xander said in a loud whisper and she hit him harder.

"Shut up, Xander."

"You two." I laughed. "Fine, I'll tell you what happened, but only because I want to know if you think I even have a chance. And if I should join the flag football team."

"Flag Football team?" Xander frowned. "What?"

"Liv told me that Aiden is joining a team and that we should join."

"She what?" He turned to Liv. "You never told me that you wanted to join when I mentioned it earlier."

"Well, I didn't decide until recently."

"Uh huh, sure you didn't." He shook his head. "So you two are signing up?"

"Perhaps," I said at the same time as Liv.

"I don't know if this is a good idea, Liv." I shook my head. "I know you think it's a surefire plan, but surefire plans don't always work out."

"What's a surefire plan?" Xander narrowed his eyes and looked at Liv. "Liv?"

"Nothing." She smiled innocently. "I just want Alice and Aiden to interact on a weekly basis, so that he can see what he's missing."

"Hmm," Xander said with a small frown.

"And she wants me to wear short-shorts." I added. "Which I don't think is a good idea."

"Short-shorts?" Xander laughed and shook his head. "That's your plan to get a man? Shake your ass in front of him?"

"I didn't know I was trying to get a man." Liv pursed her lips up at him. "But I guess I can wear short-shorts as well."

"Don't you dare," he said as he looked down at her ass for a few seconds. "Your big butt is mine and mine alone."

"My big butt?" Liv's voice dropped and I grinned to myself. It was about to go down. Xander had no idea what he'd set into motion. Liv hated her butt and I knew she did not consider his comment a compliment.

"Yeah," —his hand slapped her ass lightly— "I like big butts."

"You what?" Her voice rose and I swear daggers were flying from her eyes into his heart, stabbing him softly.

"I like big butts," he said and shrugged. "But your big butt is for me to enjoy, not every Tom, Dick and Harry on the football field."

"I do not have a big butt," she squealed and immediately started doing squats. "Take that back."

"Take what back?" Xander looked confused and I burst out laughing as Liv moved up and down with an annoyed look on her face. "Also, you're doing those squats all wrong. Your form is off."

"What?" she snapped.

"You shouldn't be bending your back like that. You should—"

"Shut up, Xander." She looked at me. "Can you believe he just told me I have a fat ass?"

"I cannot believe it." I looked at Xander. "Shame on you."

"What?" He threw his hands up with a confused look on his face. "I never said you had a fat ass. I said you had a big butt. A big butt that I like—love, even." He groaned at the murderous look on Liv's face. "Let me just shut up now."

"Yeah, you need to just stop." Liv stood up straight and stretched her arms out. "Ow." She made a face and looked at me. "My legs are aching."

"I'm not going to say you should work out more, then," Xander said with a smirk and we both hit him on the arm. "Ouch, girls."

"Alice, are you ready to tell my asshole of a boyfriend what happened with Aiden so we can all decide upon a plan of action?"

"Whoa, wait." Xander frowned. "I'm not here to help you two come up with any spells or trickery, but more to give my advice."

"We're not witches. We don't cast spells or trick anyone." Liv rolled her eyes.

"You could have fooled me," he said with a straight face. "Brock and Jock?"

"Oh, get over them." Liv shook her head and looked at me. "Are you sure you want a boyfriend, Alice? Do you want to put up with all of this?"

"I wouldn't mind." I sighed wistfully and looked over at Xander. "I know you said he can be a pain, but sometimes it's nice to have a little pain."

"What have you been telling her?" Xander winked at Liv and she groaned.

"Not enough obviously," Liv started up again and stopped herself. "Anyway, enough about you and me. Alice, I want you to talk about your story."

"Yeah, I guess." I groaned. "This is so embarrassing and almost unbelievable."

"Don't worry, Alice, there's nothing you can tell me that I wouldn't believe," Xander said. "And I've heard stories from Liv about the two of you, so trust me when I say that I can believe it all."

"Thanks." I made a face. "I'm not really sure that that's a compliment."

"Enough already," Liv said. "Xander is just looking to get himself into trouble."

"Okay," I said with a sigh and then closed my eyes. "I guess I should start at the beginning." I opened my eyes and looked at an expectant Xander and my face flushed as I opened my mouth to begin my story. The story of how I'd seduced Aiden Taylor, the older brother of my best friend in the world.

And then my phone rang. And my heart stopped beating for about three seconds as I stared. It was the call I'd been eagerly anticipating for the last six years. And I had absolutely no idea why he was calling.

Chapter Three

I have had a crush on Aiden Taylor since I was ten. Yes, I know what you're thinking, how can you have a crush on a boy when you're ten and he is sixteen? Trust me, it is very, very easy. Aiden Taylor has always been handsome. And when he was sixteen, he was the image of every school girl's dreams. His now-dark hair had been a dirty blond then, and longer, almost like a surfer's, but he'd been on the baseball team. His bright blue eyes had always been full of mischief and he'd always treated me as an annoyance, just like he'd treated Liv, but I hadn't minded. In fact, I'd loved it. I loved spending time with him. I loved it when he let us play video games with him. I loved it when he'd tickled me or played board games with us. Aiden had been the bossy older brother, but he'd also made time to hang out with us. It had been easy to daydream about him becoming my boyfriend. Not that it was ever going to happen. I was too young for him and he hadn't seen me as anything other than his sister's best friend. That was until the summer after he'd graduated from college. He'd come home for the summer with his girlfriend, Lisa, or something. I could still remember the first time we'd laid eyes on each other that summer. It had been a magical moment. I was sixteen, about to turn seventeen and he was twenty-two. We hadn't seen each other for about two years, as his college schedule had kept him away except for holidays like Christmas and even then he'd only been home for a few days.

Walking into the Taylor house that summer and seeing Aiden was like the first time you see a mountain or the ocean. It's a breathtaking, miraculous and awe-inspiring experience. But the walking into the house wasn't the best part. The best part was when Aiden looked at me. It was magical. It was one of those moments that you live to go through. Everyone should have a moment like that at least once in their life. I can remember it clearly. I'd walked into the living room and he'd looked up casually to see who it was. And his eyes had lit up in appreciation for ten glorious seconds as he looked me up and down. In that moment, I'd been Alice Waldron, beautiful swan and he'd taken in all of my glory. His eyes had met mine and for a few seconds, he'd smiled at me, with a flirtatious, sweet smile that had flipped my heart over a million times as if I were an Olympic gymnast. And then Liv had run into the room, given me a hug and he'd become his old bossy self, acting as if he had been personally assigned as our warden and we were his inmates.

I'm not exactly sure how I came up with my plan. It wasn't something that I'd thought about for a long time. I hadn't spent my years plotting how to seduce Aiden Taylor. Not at all. I think it really came to me in the moment, out of jealousy and excitement. You see, it had killed me that Aiden wasn't alone that summer. Especially as I knew that Lisa was beautiful and easy. Okay, I didn't know if she was really easy, but I assumed she was. Of course, she was sleeping in a separate bedroom, but that didn't stop them from sneaking off and making out—something that had made me extremely jealous. Then one night, Lisa had given me a note and asked me to give it to Aiden. Of course, I'd opened it and read it. And of course, I'd seen red as I read it furiously. Lisa had stated that she was going to sneak into Aiden's bedroom that night at midnight. She told him to keep the lights off and to have protection ready. She said she didn't want to disrespect his parents, but she needed him badly and didn't want to go another night without him. She also said, which made me smile, that she was sad that he didn't think their relationship was going to work out and that she still loved him, even if he was technically no longer her boyfriend. This made me grin for days. Of course, I'd seen them arguing, but I'd had no idea that they had broken up. That meant I still had a chance. Of course, I was conveniently forgetting that I was in high school still and he had just graduated from college. That seemed to be of no real importance to me. You should know that I did hand Aiden the note. And he screwed it up in his hand and threw it into the trash. I did what I thought I should do and I told Lisa that Aiden didn't want her to come to his room. She seemed upset, but accepted it calmly. I did feel a bit guilty as I heard her making a call for someone to pick her up. Though, my guilt left when I saw a hot Tom Cruise lookalike arriving about thirty minutes later and kissing her like he'd been away at war and hadn't seen her in years. Lisa left so quickly that I felt bad for Aiden, as she hadn't even told him goodbye. Well, not really that bad. And I can't say that's exactly what gave me my idea, but it was definitely one of the reasons I thought I was pretty brilliant. My plan was pretty simple: I was going to sneak into bed with Aiden and we were going to snuggle and kiss and I was going to seduce him. And it had worked. I'd snuck into his bedroom around midnight wearing nothing but a long T-shirt. I'd slipped into his bed and put my arms around his naked chest and pressed myself up against him.

"You shouldn't be here." He groaned sleepily as his fingers had grabbed mine.

"Shhh." I'd kissed his back, and ran my feet down his muscular legs. The hair on his legs had tickled my smooth skin and I'd moaned at the feeling of being so close to him. His hand ran up and down the side of my legs and he'd groaned before turning over. The room had been pitch dark and as he rolled me onto my back and kissed me, I'd been scared that he'd figure out it was me and get mad. I was pretty sure that Aiden didn't know that Lisa had left because he had gotten home late that night and gone straight to his room. His tongue had entered my mouth swiftly and I'd kissed him back with such ferocity that I'm sure he must have been shocked. He'd paused for a moment and pulled away from me and then whispered, "Damn, you shouldn't be here." I had grabbed his head and pulled him back down to me and wrapped my legs around his waist. At the time I'd thought he was talking to Lisa, but now, now I wasn't really sure if he'd known that he'd been talking to me, Alice. If he'd known it was me and he'd still gone ahead, that must mean something right? That night had been crazy and passion-filled and when he'd entered me, I'd cried out in pain and ecstasy. He'd been the perfect lover: attentive, caring, dominating and skilled. The next morning when I'd woken up, he was staring at me angrily. I can still remember the shock and disgust in his icy blue eyes. I'd gulped and blushed and hurried out of the bed, waiting for him to say something, anything, to let me know everything was going to be okay. But he'd said nothing. Not then and not ever. Not until recently. And now, well, now all I wanted to do was to repeat that night. But this time, I wanted to play for keeps. This time I wanted to seduce my best friend's brother and make him fall in love with me. And I was willing to do almost anything for that chance with him. And what I really meant was *whatever* it took.

***

"Hello, Alice?" His voice was hesitant and strong at the same time and I felt as if time had stood still. My fingers gripped the phone and my face grew warm as I realized that Aiden was on the other end of the line. I looked at Liv and mouthed, "Oh my God, oh my God" to her several times. "Alice," he repeated again and I shook my head, trying to get over my shock.

"This is Alice," I said in a prim voice, sounding like some Victorian matron from some old black-and-white movie.

"It's Aiden," he said in a husky voice and I swear to God that I would have started jumping up and down if Xander hadn't been sitting in the same room as me, looking very bemused.

"Who?" I said childishly and I saw Xander rolling his eyes.

"Aiden Taylor, Liv's brother."

"Oh hi, Aiden. How are you?" I said stiffly as I grinned at Liv who was grinning back at me. Xander was looking back and forth at our expressions with an even more bemused look and I knew he was thinking to himself that it didn't take much to make us happy.

"I'm good." He cleared his throat. "I was actually just calling to see if Liv is okay?"

"Liv?" I said stiffly. Huh? What was he talking about?

"Yeah, I tried texting her a couple of days ago and she hasn't responded, so I figured I would check with you."

"She's fine," I said and put my finger up to my lips as I looked at Liv. "Hold one second, please," I said quickly and pressed mute. "It's Aiden, he said he's tried contacting you and you haven't answered," I whispered to Liv and she frowned.

"Uh, no." She shook her head. "What is he talking about? I just spoke to him this morning."

"Oh." I shrugged my shoulders. "So he's lying? Should I tell him you're here with me now?"

"Yeah." Liv nodded. "Tell him that I'm here and that I said I spoke to him this morning."

"Okay." I was about to press unmute, when Xander shook his head and sighed.

"Do you two have absolutely no clue?" He stood up and walked toward me. "That's still on mute?"

"Yes." I nodded.

"Good." He stopped in front of me and his green eyes pierced mine. "Listen to me carefully. Do not tell Aiden that you know that he's lying. He obviously used that as an excuse to call you. You should be thanking your lucky stars, not accusing him of lying." He shook his head and looked back at Liv. "I have no idea where you are getting your advice from." He turned back to look at me. "Get back on the phone and ask him something. Be nice. Be sweet. Be happy to hear from him. Don't accuse him of lying. Don't have an attitude. Don't talk about kissing Scott or seducing him when you were 16. Stick to topics that are safe for now. Do you hear me?"

"Yes." I nodded meekly.

"I don't know why he's calling you," he said with a serious face. "Maybe he got hit in the head and actually likes you."

"Xander!" Liv screeched.

"I'm sorry." He laughed and looked at her. "But really, I think I got hit in the head as well."

"Why's that?" She frowned.

"'Cause I'm dating you." He grinned at her and she just shook her head and mumbled something. "But you know I love you. That's why I'm letting you move in with me."

"What?" I froze and looked at Xander and then Liv's pink face. "You're moving in with Xander?"

'Oh boy." He bit his lower lip and stepped back. "You didn't tell her?" He looked at Liv and she glared at him.

"I'm sorry, Alice. I was going to tell you. And it's not for—"

"We'll talk later." I made a face at her and then unmuted the phone. "Sorry about that," I sang into the phone, my heart racing as I thought about Liv moving out.

"That's okay," Aiden said stiffly. "Where did you go?"

"I had another call," I lied. "I just got asked out on a date."

"Oh?"

"Yeah, this guy I met last weekend. His name is Sylvester," I said and I could see Xander rolling his eyes as if he couldn't believe I was going down the lying road again.

"Sylvester Stallone?" Aiden asked and I laughed.

"Funny—not," I said. "I didn't say Rambo called me."

"That's good. I don't think I can take Rambo on."

"Oh?" My heart felt as if it were going to pop out of my chest then. What did he mean he couldn't take Rambo on? Did that mean he liked me? Did he want to date me? My stomach was doing somersaults.

"Yeah." He laughed. "He might not like you getting calls from guys, even if they're just friends."

"Oh yeah," I said, suddenly deflated. "That's true."

"Anyway, I also just wanted to see if you were okay."

"Okay?"

"After our Facebook chat the other day," he said softly. "I wasn't sure if I'd upset you."

"Why would I be upset?" I squeaked out.

"I realize we've never really spoken about that night," he said awkwardly. "And I wanted to apologize for what happened."

"You wanted to apologize to me?" I said stiffly. The moment felt surreal, and then the room started to spin. How was it that he was calling to talk about that night, just when I was talking about that night as well?

"I should have known better." He sighed. "I shouldn't have let it continue once I knew."

"Once you knew what?" I said softly, my face burning in shame.

"Once I knew it was you in my bed."

"You knew?" My jaw dropped. "Before the morning?" Excitement and hope ran through my veins at his words.

"Of course I knew, Alice." His voice was husky. "How could I not have known?"

"But..." My voice trailed off. "I didn't know you knew before the morning."

"I wasn't proud of myself." He sighed. "But yes, I knew." He cleared his throat. "I knew as soon as you got into the bed and wrapped your arms around my chest. Actually, I knew as soon as you walked into the bedroom. I could smell your strawberry fragrance hanging in the air as soon as the door opened."

"I, uh—I don't know what to say," I squeaked out. I had loved that strawberry spray and the matching strawberry lotion. I'd worn them both so much that my mom had asked me if I wanted to move to a strawberry patch.

"I shouldn't have brought it up. I just wanted to make sure you were okay," he said softly. "I know we're older now and we had some awkwardness recently, but I wanted to reach out and let you know that I consider you a part of the family, Alice, and I hope you know that."

"Thanks," I said softly, my head spinning. I was so confused. Why was he calling me? Did he like me or not? And what did he think about that night we'd spent together? Did he ever think about it? And did he ever think about me? Did he wish that he could have another night with me? Or did he wish that he could have many more nights with me?

"Anyway, I should go now," he said cheerfully. "Tell Liv to text me back or call me when you see her. I hope to see you soon."

"Where are you going?" I said, knowing I sounded pitiful, but I didn't want the conversation to end.

"I have a date," he said cheerfully. "I'm taking her to a Degas exhibit." He groaned. "Don't I sound boring?"

"No," I said lightly as my heart lurched.

"You're too sweet, Alice," he said, his voice sounding sexy as hell. "I just hope Elizabeth enjoys it."

"Elizabeth Jeffries?" I said lightly, unable to stop myself.

"Yes, how did you know?" He sounded surprised.

"Good guess," I said and then sighed. "But I have to go. Talk to you soon."

"Oh, okay. Bye, Alice," he said softly and I hung up. I looked at Alice and Xander and I knew that I looked like a sad case because that was how I felt—really sad and sorry for myself.

"What's wrong?" Liv jumped up and ran toward me. "What did my brother say? God help me, but I'll kill him if he was a jerk."

"He has a date," I said softly, my voice cracking.

"You did just tell him another guy had called you," Xander said and closed his mouth as Liv glared at him.

"Oh no." She rubbed my shoulder.

"And he knew it was me that night." I rubbed my forehead and then sank down into the couch. "He knew it was me, before the next morning," I said again in a daze. "I can't believe it." I shook my head and my mind went back to that night six years ago, the night that had been both the best and worst in my life. The night that I was determined to experience again. Only this time I was a woman and I sure wasn't going to sneak out of the room the next morning with anything other than a grin and a well-loved body.

"So what are you going to do?" Liv said, her eyes wide with shock.

"I don't know." I groaned. And I really wasn't sure. "I guess I'll start by joining the flag football team."

"Hold that thought, I'm going to get some a drink." Liv jumped up and hurried out of the living room. I nodded at her and sat back and closed my eyes, my heart was still thudding from my call with Aiden.

"So I need to talk to you." Xander moved closer to me on the couch as Liv left the room. My heart raced as his voice lowered and I felt him next to me. What was he doing?

Was he going to make a move on me? What sort of woman did he think I was? Did he really think I was going to let him come on to me when he was dating my best friend?

"About?" I looked up at him wearily and his green eyes looked amused as he gazed at me. Oh God, please don't tell me you want me to experience your miracle tongue as well, please do not make me have to slap you.

"What are you thinking, Alice?" He said softly, a small smile on his face as I glared at him.

"Liv is my best friend and I will tell her if you do anything inappropriate." I made a face at him and then took a deep breath. "And then she'll leave you and you'll—"

"Alice." He cut me off as he rolled his eyes. He looked as if he wanted to laugh at me. "I need to tell you something and I don't want Liv to hear. Not because I'm trying to hit on you, but because I don't want to make her uncomfortable."

"Uncomfortable how?" I asked him suspiciously.

"It's about Aiden."

"What about Aiden?" I frowned and leaned forward as my heart raced. What did he have to tell me about Aiden that he couldn't say in front of Liv?

"I think Aiden is a Dom."

"Say what?" My eyes widened as he spoke.

"I think Aiden is a dominant."

"What?" I screeched as I stared at him. My face was reddening as I thought about Aiden with a whip in his hand and me lying across his lap. Wait, could that even work? And would I even want him to use a whip? I chewed on my lower lip as my mind raced. Maybe I'd just be on his lap and he could use his hand. Yes, that was more preferable to a whip.

"A dominant is someone who takes a superior position in the bedroom and—" Xander interrupted my thoughts and I blushed as a dart of embarrassed heat spread through my body.

"I know what a Dom is." My face reddened. "I've been around town you know." Well, I've kinda been around town. I've never been with a guy that was into much experimental play, not that I haven't tried, but well it's just never worked out for me.

"Okay, Alice." Xander answered me smugly.

"Why do you think he's a Dom?" I asked him curiously, my heart racing quickly again, this time in excitement. Had Aiden told Xander that he wanted me to be his submissive? I wasn't sure what I'd say to that. I'm not exactly the submissive type. I think I talk too much and I don't take orders well. In fact, I like to order men around. Especially in the bedroom; I like to let a man know what I want very clearly.

"Shh." Xander shook his head. "Keep your voice down. I don't want Liv to know."

"Why not?"

"Would you want to know if your brother was a Dom?"

"I don't have a brother." I shrugged.

"Would you want to know if Liv was a Dom or a Sub?"

"She would tell me." I shrugged and then grinned at him. "We share all of that information."

"Hmmm." He frowned for a second and then shook his head. "Well, I don't think that this is something Liv wants to think about her brother doing."

"What?" I laughed. "Spanking women?" I winked and I was almost positive that I'd made Xander blush. I had said spanking on purpose of course. Liv had told me that Xander had a penchant for giving her a quick spank before doing doggy-style, though I wasn't going to tell him I knew that. Not in an even more obvious way, anyway. I wasn't sure that he'd be happy knowing I knew intimate details about their sex lives. At least not if the frown on his face was any indication.

"I don't know what he does exactly." Xander grinned. "But it seems like you would be into that, huh?"

"Into what?" I frowned and looked down, not wanting him to see the eagerness in my face.

"The kinky stuff." He said with a light in his eyes. "Maybe that's a way for you to entice him." He said softly. "Let him know you're down for experimenting."

"Ooh." I nodded thoughtfully. Maybe Xander had a point. Maybe Aiden was being weary because he didn't know if I'd be interested in getting down and dirty in all sorts of different ways. Maybe I needed to show him I could be a sub. Not that I'd make a great one, but I could try. And maybe I could be a great one. I was great after-all. And I had skills. Though, I didn't know if the skills I had were the sort of skills I needed to be a sub. I wondered what I would have to wear as a sub. Would he have me in leather chaps? Would he expect me to wear nipple clamps? I cringed as I thought about the pain I'd feel wearing nipple clamps. The sex had better be good if I was going to wear nipple clamps. I'd have to look them up online or maybe even go to a sex store. I'd convince Liv to go with me. Maybe I could pick up a sexy outfit or some toys that I'd casually let Aiden see the next time I saw him. I could let some handcuffs fall out of my bag the next time I saw him or something.

"Alice, you okay?" Xander's voice sounded concerned and I looked up at him with an apologetic smile.

"Sorry, I spaced out a little bit." I shook my head to clear my thoughts. I was getting carried away already. Even if it was only in my mind. I couldn't wait to speak to Liv about what Xander had told me. Though, I wouldn't tell him that I was going to tell her. I'm not sure what Xander was thinking, but how could he possibly think I wasn't going to tell Liv? We told each other everything. There was no way I was keeping this to myself. I was going to let Aiden see that I could be the best sub he could ask for and Liv was going to help me.

"That's okay." He looked at me uncertainly. "I hope I didn't shock you with the news."

"Oh not at all." I smiled sweetly, my mind racing. Xander hadn't shocked me at all. In fact, he'd just given me the perfect idea to try and get Aiden once and for all.

The end of That Night With My Best Friend's Brother. The full-length standalone novel Falling For My Best Friend's Brother will be out at the end of February. You can preorder it here!

Join my mailing list here to be notified as soon as it is released.